Séquana

The legend of the Seine

Patrick HUET

Copyright

© **Patrick Huet** august 2017

All rights reserved.

Author of the tale : Patrick Huet.
The cover is a composition of Patrick Huet and a picture of LMoonlight.

Editions Patrick Huet
73 rue Duquesne 69006 Lyon – France.

www.patrick-huet.fr

Tel. (33) 06 99 71 69 69

ISBN : 978-0-244-62775-1

Oirgin of this story.

The author of that story walked along the Seine (the river Seine) entirely on foot, from the source to the sea.

The first day of his journey, he accidentally discovered in the forests near the source a strange vestige similar to the carcass of a fossilized dinosaur. A trunk of tree felled whose roots assumed the appearance of a skeleton whitened by the years.

But the poet's gaze revealed a completely different story, the one he tells you in the following pages.

Sequana

the legend of the Seine

There are winters which carries peace and sleep, there are other which carries hatred and violence.

There are pleasant winters of whiteness, winters of snow, where the flakes are scattered tenderly over the surface of the days. There are others, alas, which bear only the cruelty of freezing.

By one of those finishing winters, when the bite of the cold weakened as the light extended, a gangue of ice emerged from the depths of a swamp. Coming from somewhere else, she had slipped over the years, from marshes to marshes, until a current pushed it towards the surface.

Raised by melting snow, the gangue diluted

slowly. So compact, so huge that the rising sun could not dissolve it as quickly as the surrounding ice. Weeks flew by. The snow had disappeared, and the grass had regained its strength, while the gangue still lay its dark, icy mass on the edge of the marsh. Under the sun, a black water, a nauseating juice that mingled with the mud of the marsh, was seeping through it.

One ends by distinguishing, a prisoner of the gangue, a silhouette to frighten the greedy senses of the leeches. And one night, when the thickness of the gangue still reduced, a tawny hand, bristling with claws, sprang from the ice which held it back. The hand attacked the rest of the gangue. A monstrous head of giant lizard appeared, abominable fangs exploded the shroud of ice.

* * *

Somewhere in a sleepy forest, a young woman of remarkable beauty awoke with a start. Her eyes, infinitely blue, vibrated with a sudden, unexplained fear.

Leaving her bed of feathers, she went to a pool

where a spring, hardly visible in this white cave, driped.

The long hair of the young lady was scattered over her shoulders before running aground on her waist like a rain of brown satin.

As soon as she entered the pool, her clothes changed into scales, as soft as cloth, but stronger than metal. A blue bird perched on the top of the pool joyfully chirped, and where the human ear could only discern a light tweet, the damsel with eyes filled with dreams heard clearly.

– Hello Sequana, hello pretty mermaid. The day is not yet risen, what is the cause of this morning awakening ?

– I do not know, Fetille. Something pierced me like a burst of ice.

– A nightmare, no doubt.

– No, it was something else. It looked as though a threat had just arisen, a mortal danger.

The bird chirped a little faster, a little louder.

– What danger could he threaten you ? In this cave you are invulnerable. No human eye could perceive it. Thanks to your mermaid's gifts, those who venture around would see a mere cliff. And you command the river, you can repress and destroy all enemies who want to approach. So why this concern in your eyes?

– It It is not for me, Fetille, that I am so uneasy.

* * *

Just as the monster had escaped from the ice, just as Sequana had woken up, a young man suddenly stood on his bed. A cold sweat wetted his forehead and his temples. The starlight filtered through the half-open door.

He went out shivering in the still fresh night.

He advanced to the end of the village, a hundred huts protected by a palisade. One of the watchmen in front of the entrance clenched his spear before relaxing by recognizing him.

– Vatrix, our bard, you almost afraid me.

– I am sorry, my friend.

– Why are you wandering in the dark ? Do you watch the moon to draw the words of a next poem ?

The bard smiled.

– I would have liked it to be so. Unfortunately, something else has awakened me.

The bard's voice, trembling with apprehension, poked the sentry, who immediately brandished his spear as he scrutinized the shifting shadows of the foliage.

– Something ? Right here ?

Vatrix reassured him.

– No, no, nothing physical, nothing material. It was in my sleep, like a blade of ice that pierced my heart, as if a terrible danger had just taken shape.

The watchman giggled softly.

– Ah ! These bards ! Always in their dreams. It was only a nightmare.

– Highly possible. Well, I think it's better for me to go back to my hut.

In the shelter of his home, he contemplated his set of stylets, sticks of paste of coal or pastel, prepared from his hands and carefully wrapped in a small linen fabric so as not to get his fingers dirty during the writing. On the table, a pile of sheets made from bark was waiting for the poet to drew his verses.

Vatrix began a text and then abandoned it. Too excited to continue, he buried a stylet and several leaves in his bag and went out again. At the palisade, the guard opened the leaf to him.

– Well, we're not afraid anymore ? I thought you had felt something dangerous ?

He did not bother to argue on this point.

– I need to move. I can not sleep.

– Well ! good walk.

By closing the access, the sentry watchman csaid in a laugh

– Watch out for bad encounters. It seems that the goblins do not like to be disturbed when they lay the dew on the flowers, ah ah ah !

Vatrix shrugged his shoulders and went to the nearby forest. He shook his head. What that he had hardly felt on his brutal awakening had nothing to do with a tricky or angry leprechaun.

"The guard is right, it's just a nightmare. It's funny, I do not remember what I saw in this dream as it is foggy... Come on, let's go for that walk and I'll forget that bad sleep ! "

A long time afterwards, when the light of dawn irradiated the curve of the sparse clouds, a great part of his anxiety had dissipated during his march. At the moment when the pink of the world slipped between the branches, he reached the source of the Sequane, as the inhabitants of that country called it, a strange name for a river. It had been called that way for generations.

It was in this clearing that it originated, just a thin trickle that quickly turned into a brook, and much more to the west, into a wide river.

Vatrix liked to follow the Sequane, to listen to her running on the pebbles in a sound so clear, so pure, that it seemed to him intermittently to perceive the song of a young lady. How strange, that his steps, today precisely, had led him to that source which charmed him so much ! On rare occasions he saw in the bounding waters the reflection of a beautifully beautiful face, and of two eyes like two slivers of sky in an avalanche of satin hair. This reflection disappeared as soon as he blinked to discover only a small ordinary source escaping from the cliff, eternally white and inaccessible that dominated the place. He had formerly tried to approach this mysterious cliff without success. The brambles around them formed bushes so tight that it was impossible to penetrate them. He had given up. About this source, however, he retained the memory of a wonderful face only perceptible at the frontier of dreams.

Sitting on the edge of a rock, he took out one of his leaves, and his hand drew :

> In the fires of the night, your gaze is mystery
> A spring burst flooded with light
> Who rests forever in the sweet secret of my days
> In the breeze of a dream with velvet perfume.

After a kiss to the parchment, he dropped him into the current that caught him and led him to an unknown journey.

Vatrix observed the leaf which was sailing on the sparkling surface until a curve took away its sight. Then he stopped minding about it, for once again he had thought seeing in the jolting of the wavelets the fleeting image of a young lady with a face so clear that it seemed crystal. A vision which disappeared in the waves as quickly as it had appeared.

It was only a dream, an illusion, and it did not matter. For even if it was only the reflection of the clouds in the water, this reflection was more dear to him than anything in this world.

So he went back to his village.

As he moved away, light fingers stopped the flow of the stream. The current returned to the source, carrying with it, back, the parchment. And the fingers grabbed the leaf before releasing the frozen water.

* * *

In the white cave, Sequana read the poem in a low voice and pressed the letter against his heart, closing her eyes.

* * *

At the other end of the country, where the forest faded to leave the field open to a series of marshes interspersed with wild meadows, the monstrous being with a lizard's head ended up devouring a carcass of roe. From his red eyes escaped flashes of hatred and fury.

He threw the last bones of his meal and leapt towards the east. The thick leather of his skin shielded him against brambles and thorns. When a young shrub slowed him down, he hacked it with a claw. Much tall than a human, his large torso could have received two adult men, one next to the other.

His fangs, as long as daggers, exhaled an uncertain borborygm.

" Find. "

He repeated these two sounds in a raucous grunt, with great difficulty, so long had his throat been unused.

" Find. Find ! "

He took again his running with more vigor, guided by an extraordinarily developed instinct.

A hill soon appeared. Muzzle in the wind, he smelled the surroundings, perceiving through the multiple scents of the bud flowers a scent of effluvium, so weak that only a particularly sharp smell's sense which knows what he was looking for could detect.

The monster belched : "Found ! Found !

The claws swept the ground with mad rage. They dug over and over again. When they touched a white mass, he slowed down his movement, cleared the surrounding clay and uncovered a long cocoon of tangled threads. From the point of a claw he cut the cocoon and examined the contents.

They were there, all of them ! Twenty green eggs spotted with red. Immediately, he straightened himself, barring a cry of evil joy.

" Find ! All ! All there ! "

The shadow of a deer stood out in a nearby grove. The monster rushed at him so suddenly that the poor beast was defeated before he could begin to escape. With a sharp gesture, he blew the blood on the eggs.

"Eggs ... live ! Saurienks, go out... live ! "

The eggs absorbed the deer's blood like a sponge without keeping a single drop in the cocoon. A strange life animated the shells. They began to vibrate. Small shocks were heard. A first one broke, and revealed the screaming head of a tiny saurian.

"Saurienk, live !" The monster bellowed.

The other shells exploded under pressure from their host. Hardly hatched, they began to fight, to bite in every direction. The enormous lizard threw at them the remains of the animal. They flung themselves on them voraciously.

"Saurienks, live. Saurienks, grow up. "

Later, the adult saurienk returned with a deer. The little monsters were now the size of a two-year-old child.

"Saurienks, eat ! When saurienks bigger, saurienks hunt with Bradax. "

He hammered his chest in defiance.

"Bradax not dead ! Bradax prisoner in ice. Bradax get revenge. Saurienks grow up and come with Bradax and kill, everywhere ! "

* * *

Far from these rivers of hatred, the bard returned to his family. In his pupils a few traces of these glimpsed reflections, so similar to the profile of a young girl, still floated.

If the clear water of the spring played tricks on

him, if what he took for luminous eyes was only the glare of the sky in the stream, if what he thought was long silky hair was in fact, the shimmering of the weeping willows, even if all this was merely chimera and daydream, he was more than happy to have witnessed it.

He had scarcely crossed the palisade, when a tall man, with a short sword at his waist, hastened towards him. Ruddy braids whipped his prominent cheekbones as he banged the bard.

– Vatrix, I was told you were out in the middle of the night !

– That's right, Ecodix. Why this question ?

– The sentry saw you take the path that leads to the creek !

– Yes, it is true, but again why so much vehemence ?

– According to him, you were heading towards the north-east !

– Where is the problem ?

Ecodix looked at Vatrix with a severe and metallic eye.

– Vatrix, were you at the source tonight ?

– You may be the chief of this village, Ecodix, but I must remind you that the direction of my steps concerns only me.

The man blushed with fury.

– It concerns me too. No one has permission to go to the source of Sequane.

– Ecodix, you set off a storm for nothing.

– Nothing ? ! While many here suspect you to go regularly to the source. An act forbidden by our law !

– Your law, Ecodix.

– No. You do not know, but a thousand years ago, all the leaders of the Celtic people met. Together, they have forbidden women water, the mermaid, to come into contact with humans. They had great difficulty in getting rid of it, by force or by cunning. The mermaid of the Sequana disappeared, like the others. Since a thousand years, she no longer exists. Her bones whiten somewhere in the depths of a pool for an eternity.

Vatrix pretended to yawn with boredom.

- In that case, why engage in such a conversation ? Why quarrel about what no longer exists?

Ecodix seizes the bard by the elbow.

- It is forbidden to pronounce the name of mermaid and even to think about it. I do it today to expressly warn you. Men have to forget that once lived, this kind of characters. Only man and the vibrant force of his sword must matter on earth. We eliminated the other rivals. And we are not going to tolerate that a dreamer, a poet, will make the memory of the past reappear. If you persist in going there, I should apply the law voted by the chiefs of clans a thousand years ago. Death for all who frequent the proscribed sources !

Vatrix looked into Ecodix's eyes. A muted irritation was lighted in his chest. A woman of a certain age ran suddenly towards them, looking uneasy.

- Ecodix, Vatrix, whatever your disagreement, I invite you to more restraint. Everyone has eyes on you.
- What did you hear ?
- Nothing, Ecodix, you were too far away. All

we have to do is to see you gesticulate to guess a fierce anger in your quarrel.

– This is our business, go your way, I still have to discuss !

– There's more serious, Ecodix. The man responsible for the maintenance of the fires left them to die. We need Vatrix and his talent to create a new blaze and allow us to cook and have heat the next few nights.

Before giving in to the emergency and seeing Vatrix leave, Ecodix whispered :

– Listen to me, bard ! Your fire lighter talent will not protect you, still wanders yourself once at the source and I personally make sure you're punished. So, do not start again and forget it !

In the central hut four people tried in vain to relight a brazier. The woman with the red-colored braids explained.

– Vélix fell asleep and the hearth died out. The logs are too wet. We have constantly struck flint against flint. The fact remains that the sparks are too weak. We cannot light anything. The village has no more fire and without it, we return to the wild life.

– The hearth is essential to our survival. Those responsible for maintaining it should be extremely vigilant in feeding it with wood.

– Fortunately for us, your talent as a poet knows how to create fire from scratch. Here, Vatrix, we brought you a seat. Do you wish anything else for the exercise of your art ?

Vatrix thanked her. He sat down opposite the brazier, took out a charcoal pen, a parchment and, after concentrating a moment on the pile of logs, bent down to write.

"On the bark of the wood a flame spreads,

Tender spouse of daylight, of the log, falls in love »

As he drew these runes, a flame appeared on the logs. It grew as the poet developed his verses to become a magnificent brazier.

The villagers present shook hands with him.

– Thank you, Vatrix, our bard. You bring us this fire through which our future is built. Of all the Celts, you are the most surprising, for you can create a fire from a few words formed on your parchments.

– I shall not always be there to rekindle the brazier." Take care to maintain it.

Upon returning to his hut, Vatrix ordered his leaflets and put a package in a begger's bag. A child passing by his door asked him:

"What are you doing, Vatrix ? More fire ?

– No, I'm getting ready for a trip.

– Where du you go ?

– In the forest, or even beyond, if I do not find what I seek. Do you see that billhook ?

The child nodded.

- I'm going to use it to cut flowers called Sarlège. They are beautiful flowers with purple petals studded with pink. I need it for the spring ceremony. Unfortunately, they are only collected on the borders of Langrevie.

– Langrevie is our country, is not it ?"

– Yes, the country of our tribe and fifty others. A considerable part of our region is covered with forests. Beyond Langrevie, we have other countries, and other Celtic villages. The most important ones are directed by both a leader and a druid. As our village is too small to have a Druid, it is my responsibility to prepare the feasts, since I am neither a hunter nor a farmer, nor a craftsman.

– But you are a bard, cried the child with enthusiasm, nd you create a fire by writing on parchments !"

Vatrix smiled at him, kissing him on the cheek. He bade farewell and moved into the forest. When he crossed the Sequane, which reached him in mid-thigh, the words of Ecodix echoed in his thoughts. So, a mermaid had existed here a thousand years ago. Thus, a handful of arrogant and vain chiefs had decided to erase from the thought of men their memory. He was still unaware of the use he would make of this information. What he was sure of, however – and his jaw stiffened – is that in no way would he dispel from his heart the image of this beautiful young lady. It was only a fragment of perception that floated today in the waters of the spring, yet this vestige, this shadow of face, was more precious to him than the assent of his companions. He would never separate from it. Even remote from the source, even prevented from going there again, he would always retain the beauty of this illusion in the secret of his soul.

* * *

Vatrix had barely go out of the stream to continue his journey on the opposite bank, and in the white cave concealed at the spring, the young beauty with long brown hair leaned over the basin.

"Sequana,tweeted the blue bird, how much alive are you in your gestures !

– He touched my waters. He has just crossed them at half a day's walk.

– He ? Do not tell me it's ...

– Yes, the bird. It's him. I felt his step as soon as he entered, just as I feel them every time he touches my waves... Today his face was closed. It was as if something was tormenting him.

– How ...? Ah yes ! I forgot you're a mermaid. You can know everything that happens in your domain.

– Yes, Fetille. I can see, I can hear, I can feel. I command this river from the beginning to the place where it flows into the sea. I can at will extend my sight from here to the mouth to discern the slightest rustling in the course of my waters. This river is my mirror. If I want to, I can also extend my hearing and hear the rabbits or doe coming to drink. Until the sea ... Yes, all that I can, for I am a mermaid, and this river is mine.

The bird tweeted again.

– Then... why can I detect like a sob in your voice ?

– Because he does not come often to the edge of my waves.

– He comes there every day.

– Only once in the day. And the hours are so long.

– It also happens to walk at the edge of the thorny clumps near the source.

– It is true, and so he approaches me. Sometimes, I almost feel that he sees me behind this image of cliff that I created to hide me.

– It's just an impression. No human eye can pierce the screen you have installed.

She caressed with a fine hand an emerald vase filled with parchment in bark leaves.

– All his poems which he offers to the current, I have them near me. When they fall into the water, it's like a kiss that lands on my cheek.

The blue bird nodded and tweeted sadly.

– Sequana, the law of men, have you forgotten it ? Have you forgotten how they hunted and captured your sisters ? Have you forgotten how, a thousand years ago, you owed your salvation only by taking refuge under this white rock ? The people of humans no longer remember you. If you speak to this bard, war will resume, for their leaders have a tenacious grudge.

– In this cave they are powerless against me. I command the river. With one murmur, I gather the water in waves so terrible that they would sweep away the greatest armies in the world.

– And they know it. That is why, for a thousand years, they have not tried to attack you. They simply banned the access of the source to the inhabitants. That is why these places have since been deserted.

– Except for him. He must be very brave to come in spite of everything.

She put her lips on a parchment and held it against her chest. The blue bird fluttered on the edge of the emerald vase.

– I know what you're thinking, Sequana. Bbe careful, however, never to leave the spring, and especially the river. Thus they were able to destroy the other mermaids. Here you are invulnerable. But as soon as you come out of the water, you lose your powers. We can capture you, hurt you and even ... kill you.

She took the bird in one of her hands and placed it on her shoulder.

– Do not be afraid, I'll never leave the river.

* * *

On the second day of his journey Vatrix had awakened at the tip of dawn. He still had not found the Sarlège Flowers and had difficulty concentrating on his search.

Ecodix's words constantly disturbed him like an irritating farandole. He was still wondering about the decision to take. It was out of the question for him to submit, then what ? To oppose the leader directly or to change the tribe ? And for which, since the other leaders had rallied the same cause ? For the first time in his life, he was intent on the possibility of going to live in the forest, away from men, and then return to settle near the spring, which was not necessarily a good idea. He ran the risk of meeting Ecodix. He was brutal but not stupid. If the bard openly left the village, he would suspect that it would be with the intention of rejoining the source at one time or another, and he would place sentinels there in anticipation.

Vatrix had never really enjoyed Ecodix. He was an intelligent warrior, absolutely unscrupulous, a cruel being who did not hesitate to kill anyone who defied the laws he had established. With his group of hunters, he protected the village from a possible external attack. Now the Celts had lived peacefully for a generation – Ecodix tended to forget it. He applied the law of the times of war with a severity which was no longer appropriate in this time of peace.

Plunged in his reflections, he paid little attention to the way. A lace concealed beneath beech leaves suddenly knotted around his ankle while a rope lifted him from the ground : an elementary snare. He was suspended by a leg, his head down.

Two individuals came out of the bushes. One of them placed a blade against his throat. The oak handle was inlaid with a ruby in the shape of a star that shone like a blood stain.

– Your goods and your riches, the brigand ordered, otherwise say farewell to life !"

Vatrix twisted suddenly, grabbed the man's wrist and threw it at his accomplice. Surprised and unbalanced, they fell into a whirlwind of dull exclamations. They quickly got back on their feet, but the bard grabbed the rope around his leg and used it to lift himself up to the branch that supported him.

– Ah, you play the cunning ! Well ! we will have fun. We also know how to climb. And you're going to spit everything you've got.

They had not yet touched the trunk that Vatrix already had a stylet and parchment hurriedly taken from his wallet. The two brigands had never heard of his gifts, for they did not care to see him write quietly in spite of their assault. It was only when an ocher blaze burst out of the first climber's clothes and knocked him down that they suspected the power of the man they were trying to rob. Far from the ideal prey they had imagined ! The second robber helped his acolyte to extinguish the flames which burned with such voracity, then pulling him by the armpits, fled through the woods.

Vatrix could not help laughing at them. He got rid of the rope and resumed his walk, watching nevertheless the surroundings.

In the evening, he had no trouble to light a fire and warm himself. He had fed up with bread and carefully-wrapped cheese, and had fallen asleep for a moment, when screams torn the torpor of darkness. Far cry, horribly lingering in the ear long after fainting.

Not being able to go to sleep again, and his heart frozen by these cries, he preferred to discover its origin rather than mope for them. In the clear night he advanced cautiously, attentive to every noise, one hand on his stylus, another on a parchment, ready to make flames burst forth in case of necessity.

Suddenly, his feet became entangled in tissue. A few words on the sheet, and it ignited the end of a piece of broken branch. In the light of this improvised torch he distinguished shreds of clothes scattered in a clearing. A more careful examination of the ground showed him a host of imprints, the claws of which had pierced the ground. Spots had soaked the humus.

"Never seen traces like these ! Nothing like wolves and bears. Perhaps some wild big cats ? they used to prowl about it, forty springs ago. One or two at most, never so numerous."

Inspecting further, a detail surprised him.

" They move on two feet, or at least what serves them. They are not wild beasts."

A flash of red light struck his eyes. A ruby in the shape of a star inlaid in the handle of a dagger !

" I now know who are the victims of this carnage. They were thieves, of course, but they did not deserve such an end.

His finger measured the depth of the claws.

"But I do not know the identity of the executioners ... Better not to go on forever."

He weighed the idea of returning to his village to reject it at once. Another smaller clan, Bramix, was within three hours of walking.

"I must first inform them of the presence of these beasts. "

The first light of the morning saw him leave the forest and along the fields cultivated by the tribe that lived there. The wheat grass licked his knees. Bramix was nestling behind a hedge of shrubs at a footstep from the Sequane, which formed a loop there. He would meet old friends, finish his picking of sarlèges and come back on.

He was already preparing to launch a warm greeting when, crossing the fence, a vision of horror chilled his gestures. The huts were nothing but ruins, doors torn away, and roofs ripped open. Spilled fires were still smoking. The ground, abundantly reddened, testified to the cruelty of the attack. Not a single human being alive. With little steps, he made the tour of the village. Everywhere the same disgusting spectacle. The same footprints that scratched the ground. He numbered about twenty different, and one last three times wider and deeper than the others. He put a knee on the ground to study it better : a monstrosity !

A shadow suddenly passed his.

Instinctively, he turned about. A small mid-man mid-lizard bounced on him, claws and fangs in front. It was not very tall, it reached only at the high of his waist, but its ferocity growled in its throat and its muscles. Vatrix snatched one of the murderous wrists in one hand, and the jaws slamming on the other. The second pair of claws cut the shoulder. The heartbreaking pain increased his strength. With a violent blow, he knocked over his assailant, who roared and leaped again. He closed his fingers on a pebble and knocked once, twice. It took no less than four strokes for the young monster to collapse, inanimate.

"His head is harder than a shield. I must go quickly."

It was too late for those in Bramix. Now he had to urgently warn his people before the pack popped up and cut them to pieces.

"I'll go through the Sequane to erase my

fingerprints and my scent, in case they are intelligent and they can be guided to the sense of smell.

Noiselessly, he made his way to the small boats. Fortunately, they had not been damaged. He untied one of them and was preparing to push it into the river with an oar. A clawed hand fell on his neck. His assailant was standing and his fangs were flashing towards his throat. With a desperate movement of the wrist, Vatrix violently stroke the forehead of the lizard with the handle of the oar . The creature collapsed on the sand.

* * *

At the same moment, Sequana wrung her hands in anguish.
"He is wounded, Fetille, he is bleeding !"

* * *

Vatrix did not understand how he had managed to get into the small boat. He had had the strange sensation that the water had raised him at the same time that he was trying to get on with it. And now, although he felt weakened by his wound, every one of his strokes of the oar carried the boat forward at a speed he had never reached.

He forgot this anomaly to think of only one thing, to row, as soon as possible, and to warn his pepole of the presence of these cursed lizards.

* * *

In the white cave, Sequana's face froze fearfully over the pool.

– He was attacked by a saurienk, Fetille.

– A saurienk ?

– He's safe now. I pushed him into a boat , and I created a current that takes him away from this place. He can go home without even suspecting my help.

The bird neglected these last words to resume.

– A saurienk, Sequana, it's impossible.

– Their species has been extinct for a hundred thousand of our years, I know. However, one of them just assaulted him from behind.

– If a saurienk had attacked him, and from behind, he would already be dead.

– It's a young Saurienk, who has not more than two days to judge by his size.

– If what you say is true, it will not stay small for very long. Their growth is phenomenal. At dusk, he will have the stature of a teenager.

– Indeed. And tomorrow he will be higher than a man, and of a strength that a human can never contain alone.

Sequana turned towards the bird a tormented face.

– I'm afraid, Fetille. The domination of the Saurienks in ancient times meant a period of abominable savagery. If they have to come back today, who knows what might happen?

– An adult saurienk possesses considerable strength, certainly. His resistance is incredible, but a troop of seasoned soldiers would come to terms with it.

– Nevertheless, Fetille, fear gnawed me.

– And why ? Your powers are tremendous, no saurienk would be able to cross the river. They can do nothing against you.

– It is not for me that I am afraid.

– Would you be afraid for humans ? For those who persecuted you, who wanted to reduce you to slavery ? For those ridiculous clan leaders who are almost as cruel as a saurienk ?

A tear ran down Sequana's cheek.

– Fear ... for him, Fetille.

* * *

Hours later, in a corner of his mind, Vatrix was surprised. While exhausted, his strokes of the oar always propelled him so quickly. How long had he spent rowing ? He suddenly noticed the familiar rocks where he was fording. He maneuvered the boat towards them and jumped.

Once it had been drawn dry, he ran to the village.

This one rested in the innocent calm which had suffused his departure. The fury of the monsters had not yet gained him. The sentinel guard in front of the palisade gave a warning cry on seeing him. Two others suddenly appeared, lifted him by the arm and led him to the chief's hut.

– Thank you, it's nice to carry me ... you know the wound, is not very serious.

For the only answer they sent him with such

force that he found himself on his knees facing an Ecodix fulminating with anger. Before he could find his voice, the hunter sent him a handful of parchments.

– What is it ? barked it.

Vatrix was about to rise. Two spears pricked his throat. He did not move. The two guards who had supported him with such celerity weared the harsh features of the executioner determined to strike.

– I asked a question, what are these writings ?

– Who searched my hut ? Who has taken possession of my effects ?

– Me. I am the head of this village, and I have the right !

– No, not that right.

– I have every right when I'm dealing with a criminal.

– A criminal ? Let's see Ecodix, the anger clouds your mind.

– You were at the source, I read it on your bark. It is much more serious than I supposed, you have not only seen the forest. You describe on your leaves the features of a brown woman "with sky-colored eyes."

These are your words, your own words formed there ! Do you deny it ?

Vatrix shook his head.

– It's the description of the mermaid that lived there. All the chiefs of the clans have sworn to erase forever their remembrance, and you, poor bard, dare ! You dare to express the portrait and describe it in your parchments. I did not think that your reflections would have led you to perceive it, even in imagination. It is an abominable crime that must be sanctioned on the spot.

– You're crazy, Ecodix. I sing the beauty of who I want in my poems. You and your peers are only stupid puppets who fear a vanished image, and during this time a real danger threatens us.

– The danger is you, Vatrix. If I let you continue your daydreams, one day or another, the villagers will listen to your poems. They will remember that at the spring there was once a mermaid

– It was a thousand years ago. You told me yourself that she no longer existed.

– The number of years does not matter. If our common people remembers her existence, they will remember many other things, they will remember the past. From the time when gigantic cities set their sparkling towers on the countryside. He will remember ... Aaahh, I'm talking too much ! This knowledge is reserved only for a small elite and only some of the highest druids are instructed about the reverse side of the scene. I have had the privilege of this knowledge only because I am totally devoted to them.

Vatrix replied

– And these two hunters now know a part of this truth."

On a movement of the chin of Ecodix, a guard answered

– Know what ? I did not hear anything, strictly nothing, and you ?

His colleague said with a bad smile

– No, nothing but a bard who moans as he rolls himself into a ball.

Ecodix had a grin of pleasure.

– My men know just enough to be able to spot the outlaws of your kind and put an end to their crime.

For the rest, it concerns only the elite of chiefs and druids.

He breathed deeply, and in a sudden voice added.

– No one, ever, must remember that mermaids existed. Only the power of men must dominate the earth. And it is that of the spear and the sword. It is that of force. I ought to execute you, Vatrix, for having even approached this mermaid in dreams. Nevertheless, you have value. I propose a pact to you. Get involved with me. With your talent as a lighter, you would be the best of my soldiers and we could conquer the neighboring clans. They will fall by the fire you create at will. We shall sujugate every nook and cranny of the Langrevie. I would be king of it, and you, the first captain. Commit yourself with me, be the best of my soldiers. You will have wealth and glory, and we will forget this quarrel today.

– You are crazy, Ecodix ! You are completly mad. You want to break the peace of the Celts and declare war. It is all the more insane that a terrible horror threatens us and watches us in the forest.

– Shut up and answer me." Are you willing to stand by me, for glory, fortune, and war ?

– Never Ecodix. Never will the gift which is mine be reduced to such infamous projects.

Ecodix stiffened, his face livid, his eyes piercing with cruel gleams.

– Since it is your choice, too bad for you, poet. Tomorrow, at dawn, you will be put to death for breaking our laws. Take off his bag and shut him up in his hut until hewill be executed according to our custom at sunrise. You will stand by his door and be vigilant. Goodbye Vatrix. An important event awaits me in the forest, and I have a long way to go.

While the guards were pushing him with their spears, Vatrix, in spite of his emotion, informed them of the threat of the monsters.

– The entire village is in danger, he insisted. These lizard men are kinds of wild beasts.

– Do not worry about that, bard.

– They've already destroyed Bramix !

– Bramix as well as two other tribes closer still.

– How? You are in ...

– Yes, of course ! Since two days. While you were enjoying yourself in the woods, survivors came to us. Ecodix discovered the base of operations of these lizards – the clearing of the Green Oak. He will go to face them tonight. It is his famous event, ah ! Ah ! Ah !

– It's madness, these monsters are too numerous, too ferocious ! Ecodix has only eight hunters, he is going to be slaughtered, and nothing will protect the village.

While making sure that the hut did not have other openings, one of the guards hooted.

– Again, this is no longer your business. Ecodix pronounced the death penalty. To-morrow you will no longer be part of this world, and the presence of these half-lizards will be indifferent to you. Think about sleeping. It seems that the last night is always the most beautiful !

And he closed the door of a dry sharp slamming, while chuckling.

Inside his abode, Vatrix cast a sadden look at his scattered belongings. Opened bags had poured tumblers and bowls in the neighborhood, and the chests their clothes. The bard began by sweeping the shambles. Ecodix had ransacked every parcel of his dwelling in his mad search for a testimony alluding to a mermaid. He had carried off not only his texts, but also all his parchments and pens. Without them Vatrix could no longer write and exercise his talent. He was henceforth only one of the most banal people and without any way of escape.

A brief smile passed over his lips. That was what Ecodix was convinced of. The ambitious warrior did not suspect that the bard had any other advantage. To do this, he had to wait for the jailers to drop their watchfullness so that they would not surprise him in his work of escape.

For long hours, he deceived the boredom by arranging his disorganized hut. His wound, cleaned and properly dressed, did not bother him any more. Ecodix had been gone for a long time. He had listened attentively to the stirring of the departure and the hoarse voice of the chief, who urged his men to hasten their steps.

"He runs to his loss, had muttered Vatrix, the

lizard men will sweep them quickly. He should have united with the other clans of the country. Together they would have formed a big army and could have got rid of these monsters. Instead, our village remains unprotected. "

He clenched his fists.

"I have to join them in the Green Oak and help them defeat these lizards by bursting fire. Ecodix does not deserve to be helped, it is to save ours that I will fight. "

Then came the moment he waited so long, that of dinner.

"A condemned man does not need to eat," cried a hunter behind the wall, while the smells of roasting reached him in the midst of strong chewing noises.

Busy eating their meals and joking in abundance, they did not risk opening the door. Vatrix rushed to his desk, smoothly pushed it away, lifted the carpet. With a bowl he began to dig. Under ten centimeters of clay, the lid of a trunk appeared. He smiled and extracted parchments and pens.

"One can be a poet and wise at the same time"

whispered the bard . In this part of Langrevie, where he was the only one to master the manufacture of writing sticks and bark leaflets, he had taken care to place a certain number of them in safe shelters. Lightning, torrential rain, or a storm could destroy its frail instruments. He congratulated himself on his foresight. However, the threat he had feared had not come from the whims of the weather, but from those of a man.

In a little bag tied to his back, he slipped parchments and pens. Then he took a leaf and a green stylus with a perfume of mint, and began to write to the attention of his guardians.

"On the leather boots, suddenly wraps

Tongues of flames with venomous fate. "

Shoutings of surprise and terror instantly broke the joyful feast of the sentinels. Vatrix hurriedly opened the door. The two men had let go their spears and tapped with their bowls on the long boots to extinguish the flames that rose towards their clothes. He did not care, and rushed to the opening of the palisade. Out of the corner of his eye, he saw the guards jumping into the pool and rolling around while howling: "Alert, the bard has escaped ! The bard escaped ! "

He forced his pace.

The river...

The boat was always lying at the place where it had been pulled. With one bound he pushed him into the water, and, once installed, began to row. Saved ! He could now ... Slang ! An arrow stood in the oar next to his fingers. A second one dashed near his ear. On the bank, the two jailers, extinguished boots and new arms in hand, were targeting him. They were already engaging another dart in their bow. He lost his stick during his race and did not have time to open his bag and take a second. He threw himself flat in the boat, his nose stuck to the bottom. The edges were not sufficiently raised to protect it completely. An arrow would pierce its ribs in a fraction of a second.

It was then that his skiff was tossed furiously as if a huge wave struck him while a rain of drops scattered around him. The bard raised his forehead. A great stir was still shaking the Sequane. There, the two guards gesticulated on the dripping grass while their bows disappeared in the water. Flatten in the canoe, he had seen nothing, but somehow the mysterious wave had disarmed them.

Vatrix took advantage of this respite. He grabbed the oars and quickly rowed down the course of the river. In the song of the water that bounced on the pebbles, he seemed to perceive a melody that had barely been formulated: "I shall always be there for you, whatever happens" and, in the mirror of the surface, the fleeting reflection of wide blue eyes and long brown hair.

* * *

– They're chasing him, Fetille. Those of his village pursue him.

The bird blew its blue-tinged featherse into chirping

– The behavior of men is always surprising.

– But these are his friends. His people ... and they want his life !

– For which reasons, pretty Sequana ?

– The huts are too far from the bank, I can not hear the speeches of its inhabitants.

The marvelous mermaid smoothed down her long hair and, kissing one of the bard's parchments, whispered "I'll always be there for you, whatever happens ..."

* * *

Fired on his oars, Vatrix jumped. Again, in the song of the water, it rustled the barely audible melody: "I'll always be there for you, whatever happens. " Definetly, his imagination robbed him of all common sense. Tiredness, his wound still painful and the frantic chain of events accumulated until he lost his head. It was urgent that he should recover and continue to advance !

Dusk smothered the light of day by degrees. The Green Oak was close now. The light of a fire played under the branches. Ecodix and his men certainly. An hearth near the lizard monsters was an inconceivably foolhardiness. They would eventually see it and attack the bivouac.

He beached the boat on the shore. The wooden bottom squealed too hard on the pebbles. Vatrix shuddered. He hoped tha nobody head. He jumped and further stabilized his boat. He was about to turn around when two shadows left the canopy. Two hands with sharp claws immobilized his arms. Two others lifted him and, in a long bestial roaring, he was taken to the campfire.

A monstrous crowd formed around his person. The lizard men came to the thorax, their jaws would have cut off a leg with a single strike of fangs. He could not get rid of it as easily as the little one this morning, if there was stil any hope.

He was fired further near the Oak. An enormous monster, twice as large as its assailants, stood near the trunk. At his side, with a sword in his hand, Ecodix wore a tense face. It was not, however, towards the dangerous lizard that his weapon was pointing, but on the throat of Vatrix.

– Ecodix, what ...?

– Shut up, bard ! What are you doing here ?

– I came to help you fight these lizards.

– Help us fight them ? Ah ! Ah ! Ah ! Poor idiot, do you think you are the only one to be imaginative ? As soon as I learned from survivors of the existence of the Saurienks and their ability to speak.

– Because they know how to speak ?

A roar rolled through the night.

– Bradax speaks ! Bradax thinks ! Bradax wants to kill !

– And Bradax will kill ! Assures Ecodix aimed at the bard. We have agreed to an appointment here at the Green Oak, and now we are allies. We'll bend this country to our will. With Bradax and his saurienks, I would have the most powerful army. It will take me no more than two moons to rule all the Celtic peoples. I will be the king, the greatest of all, and those who will refuse my reign ...

– KILL! Growled the saurienk

– Yes, Bradax. You can kill them. You can slaughter all the opponents. As I will do with this bard of my own sword.

Ecodix raised his weapon, the lizard monster stopped the blade of his claws.

– He, to be mine.

He sniffed the bard.

– Bradax recognize his smell. he, have wounded young saurienk. Bradax get revenge and eat him.

A wicked smile illuminated the face of Ecodix.

– He is yours.

– Saurienks !! You, keep him under tree ! Bradax finish talking with Ecodix. Then Bradax eat. Bradax hungry.

Clawy grips took him away under a willow tree. Near the Green Oak, Bradax had crouched. Ecodix had done the same, imitated by his men, who were five steps behind him. In the darkness beyond the clearing, muzzles sniffed Vatrix while a kind of a bad smile rolled up the chops of the monsters. Hungry gleams crossed their scarlet pupils. Bradax and the village chief, plunged in their discussion, were no longer interested in him. And the ferocious lizards who watched him lacked experience and discernment to think about stopping his hand that had slipped into his bag and now, drew words on a sheet. They did not know writing and did not associate any danger with these drawings.

"Red is the fire that arises in the evening"

A giant flame arose immediately between the saurienks and the bard. The lizards retreated, terrified by the fire. Vatrix rushed towards the Sequane. His legs split the way faster than they had ever run. A roar exploded in the clearing.

– Saurienks !! You catch prisoner. For Bradax !

Countless shout echoed through the forest. The ground vibrated with runnings that pounded the earth. The screams were getting closer. The saurienks were fast, they smashed branches and bushes under their charge.

The boat ... Vatrix was not far away, he was going to get there, he was there ... almost ... He fell suddenly. A saurienk had jumped at his legs. The bard twisted his neck in vain, for another jumped on his chest. He must have touched the river ! All his instinct urged him towards it. He struggled harder, unnecessarily ... a third lizard stopped him on the sand.

Vatrix's fingers tended toward the water. A few centimeters barely, but he could not reach it. The saurienks pulled him by the feet. He thrust his nails into the pebbles of the bank. A groove was created under his fingers as the saurienks pulled him backward. A trickle of water began to sink in the furrow and touched his knuckles a fraction of a second before the monsters hoisted him on their shoulders towards the clearing.

* * *

"They take it away, Fetille ! The saurienks ! I have to go.
– Above all, do not leave the river, Séquana, do not leave ...

The mysterious mermaid could no longer hear him. She had slipped into her field.
For a thousand years, the forest of Langrevie had not known that blaze of brown satin which was flashing in the crystalline waters of the river. For a thousand years, the banks had not reflected the dazzling blue of that gaze that propelled itself into the water, faster than a human eye could catch it.

* * *

Sequana springs near the boat of Vatrix in a stream of brown hair

Her pupils became frightened when she saw him in the midst of the Saurienks. He clung to the branch of a willow and struggled furiously, but there was no doubt that the monsters would eventually detach him.

With a murmur, she created a wave that projected the saurienks 20 meters away. The eight men of Ecodix appeared, armed with swords.

– Pull her out of the river and kill her ! Ordered their chief, who was now hurrying to the place.

Vain invectives. The mermaid, with her feet in the water, had all her power. His song provoked a second wave which knocked out the warriors. Vatrix looked for his bag. it had disappeared in his struggle with the lizards. He kept only one piece of the stylus and one half of the sheet in his left hand. As the saurienks rushed back on him, he wrote.

"Let the flames streak in the heart of the night
Let the lightning burn on the cursed monsters. "

A flood of fire fell upon the saurienks and calcined them. In the space of an instant, of this unspeakable troop, nothing remained but ashes.

Taking advantage of the gigantic flash which saturated the retina, a rapid shadow had slipped quietly behind the boat. A frightful claw hit Sequana with such violence that it propelled her to the other end of the bank. Far from the water. In three leaps the enormous saurienk was upon her. He grabbed her and swung her over him further away from the river.

– Mermaid, die! he yelled.

He was about to smash his skull against one of the trees, now completely abandoning the bard, twenty paces away. As he turned his back on him, Vatrix seized an abandoned sword and struck him at the base of the neck with all the rage of despair.

Bradax collapsed.

Vatrix freed the mermaid. A deep wound cut her shoulder. He held her head as she murmured faintly.

– The river, you must join the river.

As he lifted and turned, a familiar figure stood

between him and the shore, the sword in one hand and his bag in the other.

– Ecodix, leave us !

– Oh, no ! I have your bag and your parchments. And away from the river, the mermaid no longer has any power. She is injured. It's over for her. She'll die and you with her.

A formidable roar froze their words. The monstrous saurienk curled up to get up. The blow of Vatrix had only scarred and knocked him out. The bard could not both fight him and Ecodix and protect the mermaid. He fled, carrying Sequana in his arms. The human monster and the lizard monster pursued him. And they were gaining ground.

The river ! He had to get back the river !

A reflection on his left. He turned at once thinking finding one of the curls of the stream. It was only an error due to the iridescence of the stars on white stones. He tumbled into a crevasse. Not very far back behind him, his two pursuers shouted with joy. In a few moments they would catch him and their hunt would be over.

Just as the bottom of the ravine put an end to their fall, the mermaid's lips accidentally touched those of the bard. It was like a fire of languor which took possession of their souls. Their lips pressed more closely as their arms interlaced. Nothing mattered now, they had found each other.

A horrible silhouette of a lizard appeared at the bottom of the ravine; That of Ecodix followed him. Claws forward, the monstrous saurienk was about to strike, but Vatrix and Sequana were now paying no attention to them. They no longer belonged to this world.

Their lips united again. a fabulous wave of tangled water and fire suddenly emerged from nothing and destroyed for ever Ecodix and the lizard monster. There was nothing left. The terror of the night had dissipated forever.

For it is enough for a kiss, it is enough that two hearts in love meet to make the impossible happen.

Far from the river, the mermaid lost its powers over the water. Far from his parchments, the bard lost his powers over the fire. But it is enough that their lips join in the longest kiss to overcome the barrier of time and distance.

* * *

All you need is a kiss.

It is enough to kiss, more tender than a thousand words, a kiss, sweeter than a thousand caresses, to regain your powers.

For this power is simply the power of love.

END

Other books of Patrick Huet

Tomy's series (for children)

- Tomy the little magician and the key of the bedroom.
- Tomy at the zoo.
- Tomy and the diamond ring.
- Tomy at the North pole.
- Tomy and the baby pigeon.
- Tomy and the learned fleas.

You can get more informations here :
www.patrickhuet.net

Printed in Great Britain
by Amazon